FOR BEN

First published in Great Britain 2007
This book and audio edition
published 2008
by Egmont UK Limited
239 Kensington High Street
London W8 6SA

Text copyright © Jim Helmore 2007
Illustrations copyright © Karen Wall 2007
Music and lyrics copyright © Barry Gibson 2008
Recording copyright © Egmont UK Limited 2008

ISBN 978 1 4052 4076 5
A CIP catalogue for this title is
available from The British Library

Printed in Singapore
1 2 3 4 5 6 7 8 9 10

Who Are You, Stripy Horse?

Jim Helmore and Karen Wall

EGMONT

One Starry Night,

in a long forgotten shop,
something magical was about to happen . . .

In the tick-tock quiet, a shaft of moonlight tickled
the nose of something sleeping.
It was a stuffed and
stripy horse.

"ATISHOO!"

The stripy horse let out an enormous,
dusty sneeze and woke himself up.

He shook an ear,

then a leg,

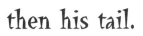

then his tail.

They all seemed to work.

"Hello!" called a hummingbird from the lampshade above. "I've been wondering if you'd ever wake up. My name's Muriel, who are you?"

The stripy horse thought hard but his mind was full of stuffing.

"Well, what do you do?" Muriel persisted.

"Er . . . I can't remember," said the stripy horse looking sad.

"Cheer up," chirped Muriel. "If you
don't know, we could try asking
Ming the Wise. But we'll have to
be careful; he hates being disturbed."

"I wouldn't upset him!"
replied the stripy horse.
"I'm very good with delicate objects!"

"Come on then," twittered Muriel.
"But we'll have to be quick.
The shop opens in a few hours . . ."

"Oops!" cried the stripy horse as he tripped over something squashy.

"Sorry!" said a low, sleepy voice.

"Stripy horse, meet Hermann," chirped Muriel.
"He's a draught excluder."

"Shouldn't you be right next to the door
to stop draughts?" asked
the stripy horse.
"Brrr!" shivered Hermann.
"That sounds chilly!"

"We're off to visit Ming," interrupted Muriel.
"Why don't you come with us?"
asked the stripy horse.
"I'd love to!" said Hermann.

"Look, it's Roly and Pitch!" said Muriel.

"They're salt and pepper pot penguins."

"Ahoy there!" called the penguins.

"And who are you, stripy horse?"

The stripy horse sighed.

"I can't remember."

Roly and Pitch studied the stripy horse carefully in case they could help. "We're seasoned travellers," said the penguins.

"We've seen a lot of things in our time . . .

but nothing quite like you."

Outside, day was beginning to break.
"Come on!" flapped Muriel.
"Time is running out!"

At the front of the shop stood a tall counter.

"Ming lives up there," announced Muriel.
"On Table Top Mountain."

They all looked up.

"How are we supposed to reach him?"
asked the stripy horse.

"Leave it to me!" said Hermann,
and he puffed
and pushed his way up, up, up.

The stripy horse slowly
climbed up Hermann's body.

"I can't look!" cried Roly,
who suddenly felt
very fragile.

When at last they reached the top, the penguins let out a cheer.
"There he is!" cried Pitch.

Fast asleep on his vase, at the top of a very grand stand, sat Ming the Wise.
Carved into the wood below him were two Chinese dragons.

"We're almost out of time! Be careful stripy horse,"

warned Muriel.

"Ming has a terrible temper."

The stripy horse tiptoed forwards.

Suddenly there was a rumbling sound . . .

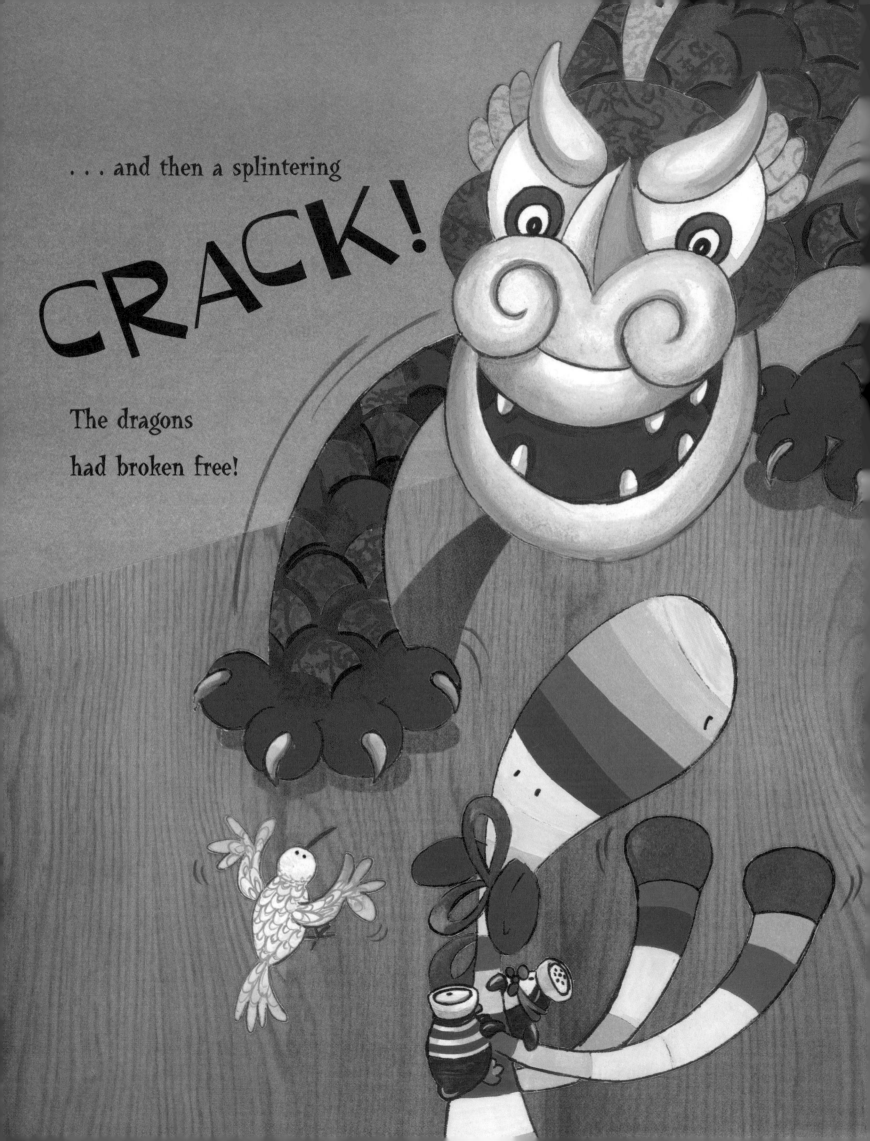

. . . and then a splintering

CRACK!

The dragons
had broken free!

"Keep Back!" they roared.
"No one disturbs the Wise One!"

"What on earth-h-h is going on?" came a hissing voice. Ming frowned down at everyone. "I'm **trying** to s-s-sleep!"

His expression soon changed to horror because . . .

Hermann had puffed and panted . . .

. . . and pulled himself up onto the counter . . .

. . . and now he was running towards them at slippery speed!

"Don't start without me!" he called.

"Oh no!"

who **bumped** into the dragons . . .

Hermann **crashed** into his friends . . .

who knocked Ming clean off his stand!

Ming's vase spun in the air.

"Don't worry," cried the stripy horse.

He moved a little to the left,

then a little to the right.

"I'm very good with delicate objects!"

The stripy horse caught Ming just in time.

"Thank goodness!" sighed Muriel.

"I've never been s-s-so disturbed in all my life!" screeched Ming.

"Please, your Wiseness," said the stripy horse, "I only want to ask if you know who I am?"

"Muriel is part of a lampshade,

Hermann is a draught excluder

and Roly and Pitch are

salt and pepper pots.

"What am I?
Do I have a name?"

Ming closed his eyes.

"I'm very tired," he yawned,

"so I'll only say this once.

ALWAYS READ THE LABEL."

And with that,
he went back to sleep.

"Always read the label? What does that mean?
Now I'll never find out who I am."
A single tear trickled from the stripy horse's eye.

"You can have my name if you like," volunteered Hermann.

"Wait a minute!" exclaimed Roly.
"Take a look at this!" shouted Pitch.

They flicked a small label that was sewn into the stripy horse's leg. The label was tatty and old but the penguins could just read what was printed on it . . .

STRIPY HORSE TOY HAND WASH

"Handwash!" The stripy horse smiled.
"My name is Handwash – and I'm a toy! At last I know who I am!"
"Hurray!" everyone cheered.

As the sun rose in the sky, the stripy horse
and his friends hurried back to their places.
The shop was about to open.

"Thanks for all your help!" he called.

"It was nothing, Handwash," said Muriel.
"That's what friends are for."

The stripy horse looked out of the window.

It was going to be a beautiful day.